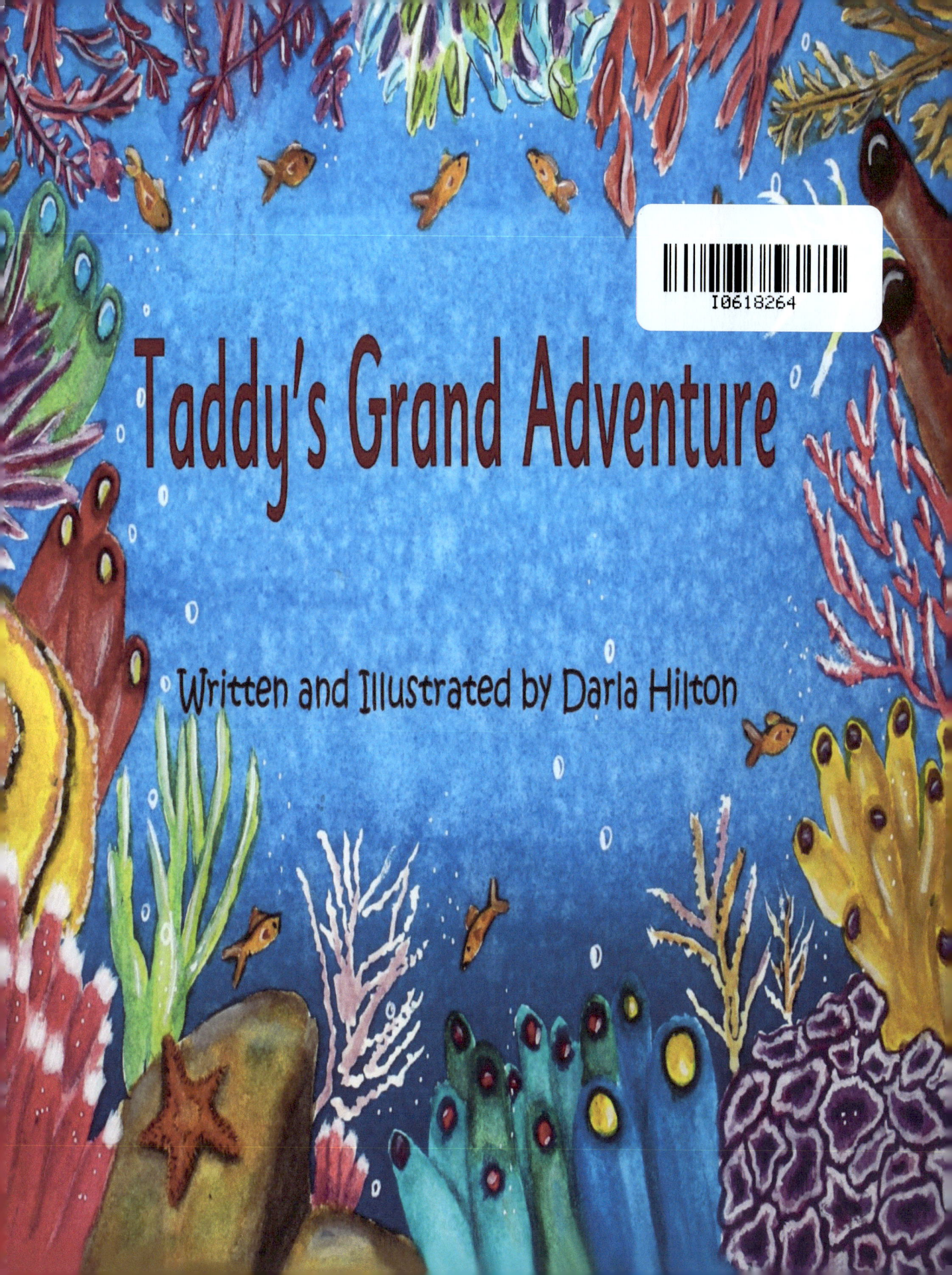

# Taddy's Grand Adventure

Written and Illustrated by Darla Hilton

For Charmi Hammonds: My Granddaughter, my little scaredy-cat.

Taddy's Grand Adventure
Copyright © 2020 by Darla Hilton
ISBN 978-1-7351481-0-6
Printed in the United States of America

Summary: Taddy is a unique little creature of the
sea. One day, she ventured out on an adventure.
At first, others met her with doubt and confusion
until she conquered their fear with an act of kindness.

About the illustrations in this book. Each page was
painted with watercolor and Gouache on hot-pressed 140
Arches' watercolor paper.

Ages 2-8

10 9 8 7 6 5 4 3 2 1

Down in the deepest, darkest part of the sea
lives a young creature named Taddy.

Taddy is not an ordinary creature, she is part dolphin from her father, and part octopus from her mother.

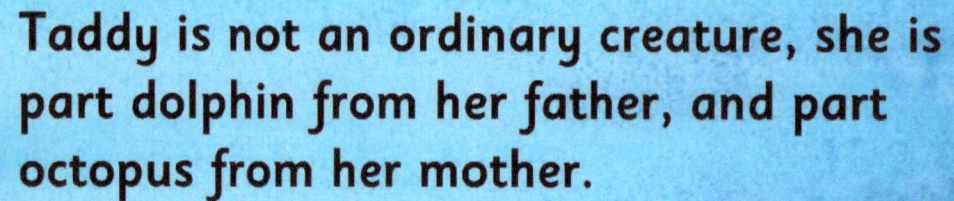

Taddy is a Doctopus. She is very rare indeed, and the only one of her kind in the sea.

Every day, Taddy played hide and seek with her mom and raced her dad to the surface of the water to see which one could jump the highest.

As the days passed, Taddy was happy and content, but as she grew older, she became restless and wanted the freedom to explore. Most of all, she wanted to have friends.

Taddy's mom and dad always kept her safe, but they knew she was getting older and looking for adventure. So, they encouraged her to go explore.

The next morning, Taddy was up early and trembling with excitement. She was ready to set out on a grand adventure.

She smiled and waved at her mom and dad and eagerly swam away.

Taddy didn't go far when she saw a group of dolphins playing ball. Without thinking, she rushed over and asked if she could play too.

They all stopped and stared at her. She heard them laugh and whisper to each other, then they swiftly turned and scampered away.

Taddy was sad and so deep in thought she didn't notice a big fish swimming her way until she smacked into him, knocking his glasses sideways.

He groaned and adjusted his glasses. With a
puzzled expression, he asked Taddy what kind
of creature she was. She explained, she was a
Doctopus part dolphin and part octopus.

The big fish curiously flipped through the pages of his thick book. There is no such thing as a Doctopus in my book; you are not a dolphin or an octopus, you don't exist.

Taddy was confused as he slammed the book
shut and shuffled away.

Then suddenly off in the green haze, she saw a gigantic fish with squinted eyes and huge teeth coming toward her.

Taddy held her breath as she frantically searched for a place to hide. She plunged to the bottom and shimmied through some tangled seaweed, hoping she would be out of sight.

She scooted closer to the bottom, as he whirled around above her. He fearlessly crashed through the water, slapping at anything in his path.

All at once, Taddy heard a clattering noise above her. There were two young octopus dressed as pirates playing with wooden swords. She silently watched as they leaped and twirled as their swords clanked together in pretend combat.

Soon some dolphins and stingrays joined in too.
They were having so much fun they didn't
notice the gigantic fish glaring at them with
angry, squinted eyes.

On impulse, Taddy pushed herself out of hiding and hurled through the water. Within seconds the gigantic fish was chasing her. She took off in a bolt of fear, taking him on a wild chase.

She rapidly swam up and down, sideways and in circles, she dodged and ducked, but with every turn she made, she could still hear the snapping of his enormous jaws behind her.

Then out of nowhere, a large fishing net swooped down in front of her. Taddy skidded to a halt, and just in time, she darted off to the side as the gigantic fish crashed into the net.

He was snarling and snapping as he twisted
and turned. The more he squirmed, the tighter
the net tangled around him.

Taddy quickly whirled around him. She used the power of her dolphin body and the strength of all eight of her octopus' arms to push and tug the net until it was tied tightly together.

Taddy was exhausted as she sunk to the bottom.
She hunched up as small as she could and hid
in a crevice of a rock.

The two young octopus rushed to her side.
The dolphins and stingrays huddled around
her, cheering and clapping.

They were so happy Taddy had saved them from the gigantic fish, and that very night they threw a big party in honor of their brave new friend.

Taddy the Doctopus
part dolphin and part octopus,
you are a hero.

I hope you had fun swimming along with Taddy on her grand adventure.
Even though Taddy was unique and different, she never gave up.
When things were rough, she continued to believe in herself, inspiring others with her kindness.

# The End

www.ingramcontent.com/pod-product-compliance
Lightning Source LLC
Chambersburg PA
CBHW041005170626
46815CB00002B/173